Keep Out, Pony!

Do you love ponies? Be a Pony Pal!

Look for these Pony Pal books:

Pony Pals ®

Keep Out, Pony!

Jeanne Betancourt

illustrated by Paul Bachem

SCHOLASTIC
SYDNEY AUCKLAND NEW YORK TORONTO LONDON MEXICO CITY
NEW DELHI HONG KONG BUENOS AIRES PUERTO RICO

Scholastic Australia Pty Limited
PO Box 579, Gosford NSW 2250
ABN 11 000 614 577
www.scholastic.com.au

Part of the Scholastic Group
Sydney • Auckland • New York • Toronto • London • Mexico City
• New Delhi • Hong Kong • Buenos Aires • Puerto Rico

First published by Scholastic Inc. in 1995.
This edition published by Scholastic Australia in 2006.
Text copyright © Jeanne Betancourt, 1995.
Illustrations copyright © Scholastic Inc., 1995.
Cover design copyright © Scholastic Australia, 2006.
Cover photo illustration by Jess Irwin.

ISBN 978 1 86504 965 6

Printed by McPherson's Printing Group, Victoria.

10 9 8 7 6 5 4 3 2   8 9 / 0

Thank you to Tess Lynch and Sarah Polehemus.

Special thanks to Janet Nickson of St. Johns Farm, fifth-grade teacher and shepherd, for her knowledge of sheep.

Contents

Keep Out, Pony!

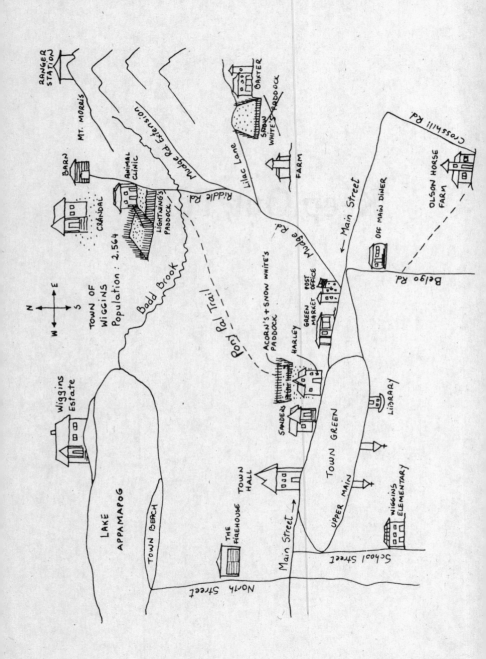

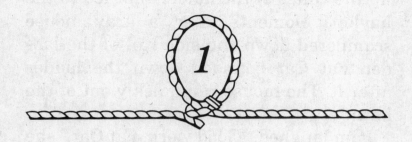

Sheep

Pam Crandal was in the barn grooming her pony, Lightning, for a trail ride. It was a cold Saturday morning, but Pam didn't mind. At least it wasn't raining like last weekend. She and Lightning could finally go trail riding with their Pony Pals — Anna and Acorn, and Lulu and Snow White. Pam brushed the white upside-down heart on Lightning's forehead. The pony whinnied as if to say, "Thanks."

Fat Cat, the Crandals' barn cat, suddenly dashed past Lightning. Fat Cat jumped up the rungs of the ladder that led to the hayloft. Moments later, a gray mouse scampered down the side rail of the ladder. Fat Cat bounded down the ladder after it. The mouse ran quickly out of the barn.

Pam laughed. "Good work, Fat Cat," she said.

As the mouse left the barn, Jack and Jill, the six-year-old Crandal twins, came in. "I just saw a mouse," said Jill. "It was moving *sooo* fast."

"Fat Cat's doing her job," Pam told the twins.

Jack looked around. "Where's Woolie?" he asked.

"He's sleeping in Mom's barn office," answered Pam.

"Woolie's a lazy dog," Jill said.

"He's just bored," said Pam. "Fat Cat has mice to keep her busy. Woolie doesn't have a job. Why don't you guys play with him?"

The twins took Woolie out to play and

Pam finished saddling up Lightning. Finally Lightning was ready for the trail ride, and Pam led her out of the barn. She saw Jack toss a stick for Woolie.

"Go get it, Woolie!" Jill shouted excitedly. Woolie looked toward the stick and then back at the twins. He didn't budge.

"Pam, he won't play with us," complained Jill.

"Dogs are supposed to run after the stick and bring it back to you," said Jack.

"*Some* dogs fetch," said Pam. "Like Mr. Olson's Labrador. Other dogs do other things. Woolie is a sheepdog. Sheepdogs take care of sheep."

"But we don't have any sheep," said Jill.

"Maybe that's why Woolie is a little bored sometimes," said Pam. She mounted Lightning. "See you later," she called to the twins.

Pam cantered Lightning across the field toward the gate that led to Pony Pal Trail. The trail cut through the woods between the Crandals' place and Anna's and Lulu's.

The girls used Pony Pal Trail as a short-cut between one another's houses. They also met on the trail for trail rides on the nearby Wiggins Estate.

When Pam and Lightning reached the entrance to the trail, Pam noticed that Woolie had followed her. "Go home, Woolie," she told him.

Woolie looked up at Pam, perked his ears, and wagged his tail. Pam knew he wanted to come with them.

Lightning whinnied at Pam as if to say, "Let him come." Pam knew that Snow White and Acorn liked Woolie, too. And Ms. Wiggins had told Pam that she could bring Woolie on the Wiggins Estate any time. "Okay," Pam said. "You can come, Woolie."

Woolie yelped happily and ran beside Lightning and Pam. But when a squirrel ran across the trail in front of them, Woolie chased it into the woods. Pam knew he would come right back to her. And he did. After that, Woolie ran ahead on the trail. "Woolie's having fun being the leader," Pam told Lightning.

Suddenly Woolie's loud bark interrupted the silence of the woods. The trail in front of Pam curved, so she couldn't see Woolie. Why was he barking? she wondered. "Woolie!" Pam shouted. "Come back." But Woolie didn't come.

Pam was afraid that Woolie was in trouble. She pressed her heels against Lightning's side to tell her pony to gallop. As Lightning was finishing the turn on the trail, Pam saw a large fenced-in pen filled with a flock of sheep. Pony Pal Trail was blocked by sheep!

Woolie was barking excitedly and chasing the sheep. The sheep were running all over the place. Woolie's barks seemed to scare them. Woolie was trying to herd the flock of sheep! But the sheep were too frightened to understand.

Pam jumped off Lightning. "Woolie," she yelled. "Come here." Woolie ignored her. Lightning's ears were pointed forward and she pranced nervously in place. Pam couldn't leave her spooked pony alone to go into the pen and catch Woolie. Pam stroked Lightning's neck. "It's okay, Lightning," she said. "Everything will be all right." Pam tried to sound calm, but she didn't feel calm. What was a sheep pen doing in the middle of Pony Pal Trail?!

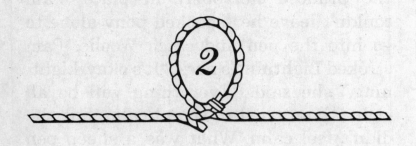

Big Questions

Pam saw Anna and Lulu riding up to the other side of the sheep pen. Snow White was spooked by the fence and the noise, just like Lightning. But Acorn was curious. He calmly watched the sheep and Woolie running around in the pen. There weren't any gates at that end of the pen. So Anna and Lulu couldn't go through it with their ponies. And the woods behind the fence were too dense with trees and bushes for them to go around the pen.

Anna shouted something to Pam across

the pen. Pam thought Anna said, "What's going on?" So she yelled back, "I don't know."

"Who did this?" Lulu shouted to Pam.

As if to answer Lulu's question, a man and woman rushed into the sheep pen. They were waving their arms and shouting. The man was carrying a big stick.

"Stop that dog!" he shouted.

"Woolie! Come!" Pam screamed. "Come!" But Woolie was too busy with the sheep to pay any attention to Pam. Lightning made some frightened grunts. Pam wondered how she could make Woolie obey her before the man used that stick on him.

The angry man and woman were closing in on Woolie. "Don't hurt my dog," Pam yelled. Anna climbed over the fence and into the sheep pen. She walked casually toward Woolie and called out his name in a cheerful voice.

When Woolie heard Anna's familiar voice, he stopped and looked at her. That gave Anna time to rush over and grab him

9

by the collar. She led the dog across the pen and pushed him under the fence. Pam grabbed him.

Meanwhile, the man was trying to calm the sheep. Pam clipped Lightning's lead rope to Woolie's collar and rubbed his back to calm him down. "Thanks," Pam told Anna. "I was afraid that man would hurt him."

"Me too," said Anna.

The woman came up to Pam and Anna. "What is that dog doing on our property?" she asked angrily. "What are you children doing here?"

"We always ride here," said Anna. She pointed to the well-worn trail that cut through the sheep pen. "That's our trail."

"Well, it's not your trail anymore," the woman said. "This is *our* property." She pointed to a new NO TRESPASSING sign on a tree behind Pam. "See that sign?" she asked. "You children are to stay away from here." She glared at Pam. "What's your name?"

"Pam Crandal," answered Pam.

"Well, Pam Crandal, I don't want to see you or that dog around here again. Do not take one more step on our land. If you do, you will be in big trouble." She turned to Anna. "You too."

"I have to walk on your property now," Anna said. "My pony is on the other side of the pen."

"Hurry up, then," the woman said.

"Anna, let's meet at the diner," Pam said.

"Okay," said Anna.

Pam led Lightning and Woolie home. She was very upset and wished that she could talk to Anna and Lulu. She hated that she was going in the opposite direction of her best friends. Pam watched Anna and Lulu ride to the paddock they shared behind Anna's house.

Pam and Anna had been best friends since kindergarten. Anna was smart and a great artist. Pam liked that Anna was always lots of fun and loved ponies. Pam

Crandal and Anna Harley thought they'd never find a friend they liked as much as each other. But that was before they met Lulu Sanders.

Lulu had recently moved to Wiggins to live with her grandmother. Grandmother Sanders lived in the house next to Anna's. Lulu was adventurous, knew a lot about nature, and loved animals. Her father was a naturalist who went all over the world to study wild animals. Lulu used to travel a lot with her father, but now she stayed in Wiggins. Lulu missed her dad when he went away, but she loved being in Wiggins with her friends and her pony, Snow White.

Pam loved ponies as much as Lulu and Anna. Pam's mother was a riding teacher and her father was a veterinarian. Pam couldn't remember a time when she didn't have her own pony.

When Pam got home she saw that her mother's car was gone. She'd have to tell her about the sheep pen later. Pam tied

Lightning to the fence post and brought Woolie inside the house. Pam brushed Woolie's golden bangs back with her fingers and looked into his eyes. He looked unhappy. "You didn't do anything wrong," she told him. "But you have to stay inside while I'm gone." She gave Woolie a big dog biscuit and left.

Pam rode Lightning down Riddle Road toward town. She had to talk to Anna and Lulu about what had happened to their trail. It would be so awful if Pony Pal Trail was *ruined*!

Pam remembered the first time she and Anna discovered the trail. A few days before they started second grade, they were playing catch in the Crandals' field. One of Pam's tosses went over Anna's head and the ball landed in the woods. The girls went after the ball and found it at the beginning of a trail they'd never seen before. The two girls followed the trail for a little ways. "I wonder where it goes?" Anna said.

14

"Me too," said Pam. "But we better go back now. My mother said to stay in the field."

"Let's tell her about this trail!" said Anna.

Pam's mother was interested in the trail, too. So the next time Anna came for a visit, Mrs. Crandal and the girls went for a hike. They walked for half an hour before the trail ended. Anna and Pam couldn't believe their eyes. The trail stopped right behind Anna's house!

That day Anna and Pam decided it was their secret trail. Their parents agreed that they could use the trail to walk to each other's houses. And last year, when Anna finally had her own pony, they began using their secret trail to *ride* back and forth to each other's houses. That's when they named it Pony Pal Trail. Pam thought being a Pony Pal wouldn't be the same without Pony Pal Trail.

Pam and Lightning reached Belgo Road. They made a left and rode up to Off-Main

Diner. Acorn and Snow White were already hitched to the post. Pam tied Lightning beside them, gave each of the ponies a loving pat, and went inside. Because Anna's mother owned the diner, the Pony Pals helped out by being their own waiters. Lulu was carrying a tray with a pitcher of milk and three glasses toward their favorite booth. Anna carried a plate of brownies. Pam dropped into the booth. The three of us have solved a lot of problems, Pam thought. But how are we going to solve *this* one?

Bad News

The moment the girls sat down in the booth, they started talking all at once.

"Who were those awful people?" asked Lulu.

"Why were they so mean to Woolie?" said Pam.

"When did they put up that fence?" asked Anna.

Pam put her hands up. "Wait a second," she said. "Let's talk one at a time. Lulu, you go first."

"Who are those mean people?" asked

Lulu. "Have you ever seen them before, Pam?"

"Never," answered Pam.

"Maybe they just moved to Wiggins," said Anna. "Maybe they bought that land."

"And put a sheep pen there," added Pam.

"But when did they put in that fence?" asked Lulu. "We ride there all the time. We would have noticed it."

"We didn't ride last weekend because it was raining," Pam reminded her friends.

"And I didn't ride out there at all during the week," added Lulu.

"So we haven't been on the trail for over a week," Pam said.

"They could have built that fence in a week," said Anna. "My dad and brother put in our paddock fence in two days. It would be so awful if they *really* own part of Pony Pal Trail. They were so mean."

"What if we can never use the trail again?" asked Pam sadly.

"We can't let that happen," said Lulu. "We have to solve this problem."

"How?" asked Pam.

"First, we should find out who they are," suggested Lulu.

"And if they *really* own the land," added Anna.

"How are we going to do that?" asked Lulu.

The three girls thought for a minute.

"I know," said Pam. "Let's go over to Baxter Realty. Mrs. Baxter might know."

"It's a place to start," said Anna.

Pam and Lulu cleared the table while Anna went back to the kitchen to find some carrots. After they gave the carrots to their ponies, they went next door to Baxter Realty.

The girls could see Mrs. Baxter sitting at her desk near the front window. They ran up the steps and walked into the office.

"Hi, girls," Mrs. Baxter said cheerfully. "I noticed your pretty ponies out there." Then she frowned. "My, you three don't look very happy today. What's happened?"

Pam explained about the sheep pen they found on Pony Pal Trail.

"We thought you might know if somebody bought part of our trail," said Anna.

"And who they are," added Lulu.

"There was a house for sale out on Riddle Road," said Mrs. Baxter. "I'll look it up." Mrs. Baxter tapped some keys on her computer and watched the screen. "Here it is," she said. "Stephen Stewart and Cynthia Prindle Stewart purchased twelve acres and a house from a Julie Rosen two weeks ago. Now let's look up that property on a map and see if it includes part of your trail."

"Maybe they don't own the trail," said Lulu. "Then we could make them move the sheep pen."

Pam crossed her fingers.

Mrs. Baxter pulled a map out of her file

drawer and laid it on the desk. The girls gathered around to study it.

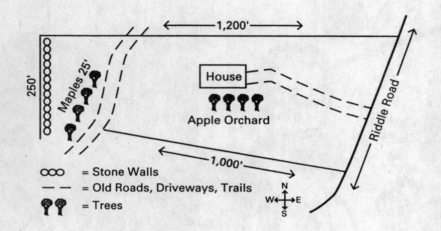

"There's Riddle Road," Pam said.

"Look! And there's a house way back here," said Anna.

"There's a mailbox for that house on Riddle Road," said Pam. "I've seen it."

Lulu pointed to a double dotted line that went through the back part of the Stewarts' property. "I bet that's Pony Pal Trail," she said.

Mrs. Baxter studied the map. "I'm afraid it is, girls," she said. "A double dotted line is the symbol for old roads, driveways, and trails."

"And look at those tree symbols," said Anna. "There are big maple trees on that side of the trail."

"I guess Julie Rosen didn't mind that you were riding on her land," said Mrs. Baxter.

"She was nice to us," said Anna.

"Everybody in Wiggins is friendly about that sort of thing," said Pam.

"Everybody but the Stewarts," complained Lulu.

"Why couldn't they put their sheep pen someplace else?" Anna asked.

"They must have decided that's the best spot for it," said Mrs. Baxter. "It *is* their land."

"But why did they have to be so mean to us?" asked Pam.

"People can be very touchy when it comes to other people trespassing on their property," said Mrs. Baxter. "I'm sorry to give you such bad news."

The phone rang. "I better get back to work," she said.

" 'Bye," said Lulu.

"Thank you," said Anna and Pam in unison.

The girls left Baxter Realty and went back to their ponies.

"What are we going to do?" groaned Lulu.

"The Stewarts are ruining everything," said Pam.

"Why don't we make our trail go around the sheep pen?" suggested Anna. "It'll just be a little longer."

"I already thought about that," said Pam. "The bushes are very thick on the other side of that fence. There's a rock ledge back there, too. We can't make a path around it."

"Besides," said Lulu. "The Stewarts own some of that land, too. I saw it on the map."

"It's hopeless," said Pam.

"We can't give up," said Anna.

"I think we should write the Stewarts a letter and explain everything to them," said Lulu.

"That's a good idea," said Anna. "Let's go back to your place, Pam, and write it on your mother's computer."

"Okay," said Pam.

But she wasn't sure a letter would save Pony Pal Trail.

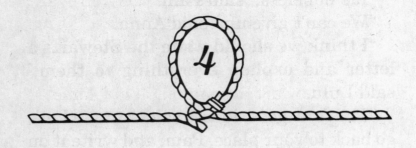

Where's Woolie?

The Pony Pals rode up to the Crandals' barn. Mrs. Crandal and a riding student were leading out Daisy, a school pony, from the barn.

"There you are, Pam," Mrs. Crandal said. "I was looking for you."

"Mom, wait until you hear what happened to us," said Pam excitedly. "It's really *awful*."

"I've already heard about it on my answering machine," Mrs. Crandal said. "Cynthia

26

Stewart left me a message. Do you want to explain what happened?"

"We didn't do anything wrong," said Lulu.

"Mrs. Stewart is so mean," said Anna.

"Mom, what happened was —" Pam started saying.

"I have a lesson with Lydia," Mrs. Crandal told the girls. "And two more lessons after that. You can tell me your side of the story later." She walked toward the riding ring with Daisy and Lydia.

Just then, Jack and Jill appeared around the corner of the barn. "Where's Woolie?" Jill asked Pam.

"In the house," said Pam.

"No, he's not," said Jill.

"We can't find him anywhere," said Jack. "He disappeared."

"Maybe he's lost," said Jill sadly.

The Pony Pals looked at one another. They knew where to find Woolie.

"He's probably on Pony Pal Trail," Anna told the twins.

"We'll go out with our ponies and bring him back," said Pam.

The Pony Pals cantered their ponies across the field. Pam led the way on the trail. She remembered how the Stewarts said they'd call the police if they saw the dog or the girls on their property again. She urged Lightning to go faster. "Come on, Lightning," she said. "Do it for Woolie."

Lightning twitched his ears as if to say, "Okay," and rushed forward.

When they reached the big turn in the trail, Pam halted Lightning. The Pony Pals dismounted.

Pam handed Lightning's reins to Anna. "I'll sneak up on foot and see if Woolie's there," she whispered. She rubbed the upside-down heart on Lightning's forehead for good luck and left her pony and friends.

Pam snuck through the woods until she had a view of the sheep pen. All the sheep

were in one corner. Woolie was in the pen, too. He was calmly walking beside the flock of sheep like a guard. This time the sheep weren't trying to run away from him. Pam looked around. She didn't see the Stewarts anywhere.

Pam climbed over the fence and walked toward Woolie. She held the lead rope behind her back and spoke calmly. "Hi, there, Woolie," she said. "You're doing a good job taking care of these sheep. But it's time to go now." She clipped the lead rope onto Woolie's collar.

A car door slammed shut. The Stewarts? Pam heard the voices of a man and woman. "Hurry," Pam told Woolie. She ran him all the way back to her friends. "The Stewarts are here," she whispered breathlessly. "Let's get out of here."

"You go first with Woolie," Lulu told Pam. "We'll follow."

The twins were waiting for the girls in the paddock. They hugged and kissed Woolie.

"Don't let him off the lead until you bring him into the house," Pam told them. "And don't let him out again."

The girls cooled down their ponies, gave them water and apples, and let them out into the paddock. Then they went into Pam's house. Jack and Jill were in the kitchen with Woolie. Pam told the twins to put fresh water in Woolie's dish and give him a bone.

"He's a bad dog," said Jill. "He ran away."

"He's not a bad dog," Pam said. "He just wanted to take care of some sheep he found."

"But the people who own the sheep don't want him to go on their land," explained Lulu.

"So we have to keep him in the house or the barn for a while," added Pam. "And anytime he's outside he has to be on a leash."

"That's awful," said Jack.

"Poor Woolie," said Jill.

31

The Pony Pals went to the barn office to write a letter to the Stewarts. When they finished, Pam read it out loud.

Dear Mr. and Mrs. Stewart:

We are sorry that we scared your sheep this morning. We didn't know that you bought that land. And we didn't know you had sheep. Woolie is a sheepdog. He wanted to take care of the sheep. He wouldn't hurt them. Woolie wouldn't hurt anyone.

We have been riding on that trail for a long time. Mrs. Rosen didn't mind. A lot of people in Wiggins let us ride our ponies on their land. We are very careful and don't hurt anything. Our ponies are very well-behaved.

We would like to have a meeting with you to talk about this problem.

Thank you.

Sincerely,

Pam Crandal
Anna Harley
Lulu Sanders

P.S. You can write back to us at the Crandals.'

"I think it's a good letter," said Lulu.

"Let's go put it in their mailbox right now," said Anna.

The girls ran down Riddle Road and put the letter in the Stewarts' mailbox. "I hope this works," said Lulu.

"It *has* to," Anna said.

"Or it's the end of Pony Pal Trail," added Pam sadly.

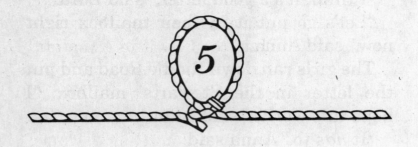

The Letter

Pam checked the Crandals' mailbox after school on Monday. The mailbox was empty. Maybe Mom already got the mail, Pam thought. She went into the house to find her mother. "Did I get any mail today?" Pam asked.

"No," answered her mother "But I received a fax today from our new neighbors. Did you write the Stewarts a letter?"

"Yes," said Pam. "The Pony Pals did."

"That's what I thought," said Mrs. Crandal.

She handed Pam a fax. Pam read it quickly. The letter from the Stewarts upset her. She had to show it to Anna and Lulu.

"I have to ride over to Lulu's and Anna's right away," Pam told her mother. She held up the fax letter from the Stewarts. "We have to figure out what to do."

"You girls will have to stay away from the Stewarts' land," Mrs. Crandal said. "We don't want to have trouble with our new neighbors. I'm having enough trouble keeping Woolie from going back there."

"They're ruining Pony Pal Trail," said Pam.

"I know," said Mrs. Crandal. "But it is their property, Pam."

"I know, Mom," Pam said. "But I still have to talk to the other Pony Pals. I'm going to ride over there now. Okay?"

"You can't go on Pony Pal Trail," her mother reminded her.

"I'll go on Riddle Road," said Pam.

"It's too far that way," Mrs. Crandal

said. "It gets dark early now. And you're not allowed to ride in the dark. Call them instead."

Pam went to phone her friends. Lulu was at Anna's house, so the girls had a Pony Pal phone meeting.

First Pam read Lulu and Anna the fax.

Dear Dr. and Mrs. Crandal:

My husband and I recently moved to Wiggins. Our flock of fourteen sheep are in a pen we built at the back of our property. This past Saturday we had an unfortunate incident with your daughter. She and her friends came onto our property on horseback. They wanted to cross through the pen on their horses. An unleashed dog accompanied them. The dog barked ferociously and chased our sheep.

Dr. Crandal, I'm sure you know that frightened sheep can run themselves to death. Also, we have two pregnant sheep. It is especially dangerous for them to be chased around the pen.

My husband and I go to work during the day. We cannot supervise our flock all the time. You must keep your dog at home. And the girls and their horses are not allowed to cross our land. They must keep out.

Please be firm with your child.

Sincerely,

Cynthia Prindle Stewart

Pam finished reading. "I hate that she wrote to my parents instead of to us," she said. "We're the ones who wrote to her."

"She's the kind of adult who thinks kids don't know anything," said Lulu.

"She didn't even mention the trail," said Anna.

"We need to figure out what to do next," said Lulu. "Why don't you come over here, Pam?"

"My mother said it's too late," said Pam. "I can't use Pony Pal Trail and it takes too long on the roads."

"We have to get our trail back," said Anna.

"It's time for three ideas," said Lulu.

"Let's all work on our ideas tonight," said Anna. "We can share them before school tomorrow."

Pam was too upset to say anything.

"We're not giving up, Pam," said Lulu softly.

"I know," said Pam. She said good-bye to her friends and hung up the phone.

Pam felt like crying. Anna and Lulu lived right next door to each other. She would be the one who would be left out. If we lose Pony Pal Trail forever, Pam thought, I'll always be left out.

Pam wanted to see the one friend she could always count on when she was sad. She put on her jacket and hat and went to the barn.

When Lightning saw Pam, the pony galloped across the paddock toward her. "Oh, Lightning," Pam cried. She leaned against her pony's side and sobbed. Lightning nickered softly as if to say, "It's all right. I'm here. I'm your friend."

"Lightning, what are we going to do?" Pam asked. "Pony Pal Trail is ruined forever."

Lightning shook her head and whinnied. To Pam she seemed to be saying, "Don't give up. The Pony Pals never give up."

Pam fed Lightning her oats and brought her inside for the night. Then she went back to her room to work on the Pony Pal Trail problem. Lightning was right. She couldn't give up.

6

Three Ideas

The next morning the Pony Pals met at their lockers to share their ideas. "I worked on this idea for a long time," Pam told her friends. "It's not good enough to solve the problem. But maybe it will help."

"What is it?" asked Lulu.

Pam opened her notebook and read her idea:

Woolie can watch and protect the Stewarts' sheep when the Stewarts are at work.

"But Woolie scares the sheep," said Lulu. "He might hurt them, especially the pregnant ones."

"I looked up sheep and sheepdogs in our CD-ROM animal encyclopedia. And I talked to my dad about them," Pam said.

"What did you learn?" asked Lulu.

"It takes sheep a while to get used to a new sheepdog," said Pam. "The sheep were scared because they didn't know Woolie."

"Woolie was just trying to be a good sheepdog," said Anna.

"That's right," said Pam. "And guess what?"

"What?" asked Anna and Lulu together.

"When I found Woolie with the sheep the other day," Pam said, "the sheep weren't running away from him. I think the Stewarts' sheep are already used to Woolie."

"Watching the sheep during the day would be a perfect job for him," said Lulu.

"But how are we going to tell the Stewarts that?" asked Pam. "They won't even talk to us."

"That's where my idea can come in," said Lulu. She handed a slip of paper to Anna. Anna read Lulu's idea out loud.

Do something nice for the Stewarts.

"They've been so mean to us," Anna said. "Why should we be nice to them?"

"If we are nice to them, maybe they'll be nicer to us," said Lulu.

"But what can we do for them?" asked Pam.

"I didn't figure that part out," said Lulu. "We have to work on it."

The warning bell rang for homeroom.

"We have to go," said Pam.

"Quick, Anna," said Lulu. "What's your idea?"

Anna flipped open her art pad and showed Lulu and Pam a drawing.

"My dad said he'd build two new gates in the Stewarts' fence for free," said Anna. "We could go right through the pen that way."

"I read that sheep and horses are good companions," said Pam. "Our ponies wouldn't bother the sheep."

"If there were two more gates in the fence, we could use all of Pony Pal Trail again," said Anna.

"*If* the Stewarts let us ride through their property," said Lulu.

"And *if* they will let us put in gates," added Pam. "Those are two big *ifs*."

"That's why we have to think of something nice to do for them," said Lulu.

The second bell rang. It was time to go to class.

After school the girls walked to the diner together.

"What nice thing can we do for the Stewarts?" asked Lulu.

"Maybe we could give them a present," said Pam.

"Like what?" asked Anna.

"You could make a drawing of their sheep," Lulu told Anna. "We could put it in a pretty frame and everything."

"They'd have Anna arrested if she went there to draw," Pam said. "We'd just get in more trouble."

"I have an idea," said Anna. "We could have a party and invite them."

"They wouldn't want to go to a party with kids," said Pam.

"We'd only invite grown-ups," said Lulu. "We'd be the only kids."

Pam didn't feel like making a party for the Stewarts. But she knew it might be a way of getting Pony Pal Trail back. Maybe it would work.

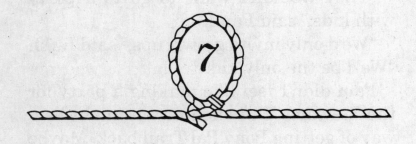

Guess Who?

The Pony Pals were walking up to the diner steps. Anna suddenly grabbed Pam's arm. "Look," she whispered.

Pam saw Mrs. Stewart coming out of the diner. Lulu saw her, too. "Be nice to her," Lulu whispered.

Pam stepped in front of Mrs. Stewart. "Hello, Mrs. Stewart," Pam said in her friendliest voice. "I'm Pam Crandal."

"Hi," said Lulu. "I'm Lulu Sanders."

"And I'm Anna Harley," said Anna. "We're so glad to see you."

Mrs. Stewart looked at the girls with surprise. "Did Mrs. Crandal give you my message?" she asked sternly. "You are not to bother my sheep again."

"She told us," said Pam.

"Then why are you glad to see me?" Mrs. Stewart asked.

Anna and Lulu didn't know what to say. They looked at Pam for the answer. "We're glad to see you because . . . because my mother is having a tea party," said Pam. "And she asked us to invite you and Mr. Stewart."

Anna smiled at Pam. And Lulu made a small "okay" sign with her fingers.

"It's a party to welcome you and your husband to Wiggins," said Lulu.

"And introduce you to some of your new neighbors," added Anna.

"We'll be there, too," said Anna. "We're helping."

"But we'll be the *only* kids," said Pam. "It's a party for grown-ups."

"When is this gathering?" asked Mrs. Stewart.

Lulu and Anna looked at Pam again. "Ah-h . . . Sunday . . . at four o'clock," answered Pam.

Mrs. Stewart smiled at the girls for the first time. "Thank your mother for inviting me," said Mrs. Stewart. "Tell her that Mr. Stewart and I will be happy to come by for tea." She turned and walked down the steps.

The Pony Pals rushed into the diner and ran to their favorite booth.

"Did you see that?" said Lulu. "She actually *smiled* at us. Pam, that tea party idea was so great."

"But who will we invite?" asked Pam.

"What if your mother won't let us have a party?" asked Lulu.

"I've never even been to a tea party," exclaimed Anna.

Lulu held up her hands. "Slow down,"

she said. "First things first. Pam, call your mother and see if it's okay to have the party."

Pam went to the pay phone in the back of the diner. A few minutes later she was back at the booth. "My mother said we could have the party," Pam told Anna and Lulu. "But she teaches until four o'clock on Sunday, so we have to do all of the work."

"That's okay," said Lulu.

"Let's invite Ms. Wiggins," Anna said.

"She's in Paris this week," Pam reminded Anna.

"Who else can we invite?" asked Lulu.

"We should invite your grandmother and my parents," said Pam.

"With the Stewarts, that's seven adults," said Lulu. "That will be plenty of people."

"But how do you make a tea party?" asked Anna.

"I went to lots of tea parties when I lived in England," Lulu said. "I know just what to do. First, we'll make a list of what we're going to serve."

Pam took out paper and a pencil.

"We should have a cake," said Lulu. "It's always nice to have a cake at a tea party."

"We could make a cake that's shaped like a lamb," said Anna. "The Stewarts would love that."

"Perfect!" said Pam and Lulu in unison.

"And we should make cucumber sandwiches," said Lulu. "We'll cut them into quarters. Sandwiches at tea parties are always small."

Pam and Anna had never had cucumber sandwiches, but Lulu promised them that adults loved them at a tea party. Soon they were finished with the menu.

MENU FOR THE STEWARTS' TEA PARTY

CUCUMBER SANDWICHES
A LAMB CAKE
BROWNIES
CANDY
FRUIT PUNCH
TEA

"My mother will let us have brownies from the diner," said Anna, "so we don't have to make those."

"And cucumber sandwiches are easy to make," said Lulu.

"We can make the cake Sunday morning," said Anna.

"My kitchen is the biggest," said Pam. "Let's do it there."

"It's going to be the best tea party ever," said Lulu.

"By the time it's over, the Stewarts are going to say that we can put gates in their pen," said Anna.

"And they'll let Woolie watch their sheep," said Pam.

"And we'll have Pony Pal Trail back," added Anna.

Everything depends on this tea party, Pam thought.

Pony Pal Tea Party

By four o'clock on Sunday afternoon, everything was ready for the tea party.

The girls had put out Mrs. Crandal's best china cups and plates, the platter of small sandwiches, a pitcher of fruit punch, and plates of brownies and candies. The lamb-shaped cake was in the center of the table. It was frosted with curls of creamy white frosting and had black licorice eyes and nose and a red licorice mouth. A big kettle of water was heating up on the stove for tea.

Pam tied a red scarf around Woolie's neck. "Be on your best behavior," Pam warned him. "We're trying to get you a job."

The doorbell rang. "I hope that's not the Stewarts," said Pam. "We're the only ones here."

Lulu opened the front door. It was her grandmother and Anna's father. Anna's mother was too busy at the diner to attend the party. Lulu led them into the living room. A few minutes later Mrs. Crandal and Dr. Crandal came in. The Crandal twins and Woolie were in the living room, too. Everyone was waiting for the Stewarts.

"We have five kids and four adults," Pam whispered to Lulu and Anna. "I hope the Stewarts don't think that's too many kids."

"I just wish they'd get here," said Lulu.

The phone rang. Mrs. Crandal went to the kitchen to answer it. She was back in a minute. "I have bad news for you," she told the Pony Pals. "The Stewarts can't come to your party. One of their sheep is delivering a lamb and they don't want to leave her."

"Do they need me?" Dr. Crandal asked.

"So far things are going normally," Mrs. Crandal told her husband. "But Mrs. Stewart said that she would call if they do have problems."

"Why didn't Mrs. Stewart tell us earlier that they couldn't come?" asked Pam.

"A shepherd doesn't know *exactly* when a lamb will be born," said Dr. Crandal. "You know that, Pam."

"Mrs. Stewart sounded very nice on the phone," Mrs. Crandal told the girls.

"She hasn't been very nice to us," said Anna.

The girls did their best to make a nice party for the guests who had come. But Pam kept thinking that the tea party wasn't going to help them get Pony Pal Trail back.

That night the Pony Pals were having a

barn sleepover at Pam's. At nine-thirty they went out to the paddock to say good night to their ponies. Then they went to the barn office and crawled into their warm sleeping bags. But they didn't go right to sleep.

"What are we going to do about Pony Pal Trail?" Pam asked.

"I guess we should think of something else to do for the Stewarts," said Lulu.

"The tea party was such a good plan," said Pam. "I wish they had come to it."

"I keep thinking about that newborn lamb," said Anna. "It must be so cute."

"I'd like to see it," said Lulu.

"Me too," said Pam. "But we can't go over there. They said to keep off their property."

"We don't have to go on their property to see the lamb," said Lulu.

"They can't tell us not to ride on the parts of Pony Pal Trail they don't own," said Anna.

"We don't have school tomorrow because of the teachers' meetings," said Lulu. "And the Stewarts will be at their jobs."

"It's a perfect time for us to see the lamb," added Anna.

"Maybe we'll have some new ideas about how to save Pony Pal Trail when we're there," said Pam.

The next morning the girls fed their ponies and went to the house for breakfast. Then they saddled up the ponies for a trail ride to see the newborn lamb.

"This will be fun," Pam told Lightning as she tightened the girth. "You love baby animals."

Anna led the way onto the trail. "Come on, Acorn," she said. "Let's ride." Acorn took off. Snow White and Lightning followed.

The Pony Pals were soon at the turn in the trail just before the sheep pen. "Let's lead our ponies the rest of the way," suggested Pam.

Anna saw the lamb first. It was staying as close to its mother's side as possible. "It's so cute," said Anna.

"Let's go closer," said Pam.

The girls tied their ponies to trees and walked along the fence. "Look!" said Lulu excitedly. "There's *another* baby lamb."

Pam saw a ewe lying on the ground near her mother. "It's a newborn!" whispered Pam. "See, the mother is licking it clean." The girls walked along the fence line to have a better view.

"There's *another* baby," said Anna. "Near the mother's back leg."

"She had twins!" exclaimed Pam.

"And the Stewarts probably don't even know," said Lulu. "It's a good thing the ewe didn't have problems."

"We should hang around here and keep an eye on them," said Pam. "Just to be sure nothing goes wrong now."

Lightning nickered. "Lightning wants to see the babies," said Anna.

Pam noticed that Lightning was pulling

on her lead rope and dancing nervously in place. "I think she's still spooked by the fence," said Pam. She walked over to her pony. "Everything is okay," she told Lightning. "You were here the other day. It's just a new fence." Pam untied Lightning's rope and walked her along the fence line. "You have to get used to this fence," she told her pony.

Lightning lowered her head and sniffed the ground as she followed Pam along the fence. "That's right, Lightning," Pam said. "It's just a fence."

Suddenly Lightning stopped. She tried to reach her nose under the lowest rung of the fence. Then she whinnied softly and pawed the ground. The bush moved.

"Anna, Lulu," Pam called. "Come here. Lightning's found something."

One, Two . . . Three

Anna and Lulu rushed over to Pam and Lightning. Pam pointed at the bush on the other side of the fence. "Something is in there," she said.

The bush moved again.

"I wonder what it is," said Anna.

"I'll go look," said Lulu. She climbed into the pen and bent over the bush. Just then the girls heard a weak, bleating sound. *"Maa-maa. Maa-maa."*

"It's another newborn lamb!" whispered Lulu excitedly. "It's caught in the bush."

"We can't worry about trespassing now," Pam said. "The Stewarts would want us to help their lamb." Anna held Lightning's lead rope while Pam went into the pen with Lulu.

Pam saw a tiny lamb curled up in the branches. It was still wet from being born. She knelt in front of it. "We have to free it," she told Anna and Lulu. "It will die without its mother."

Pam put her hands around the trembling lamb as Lulu moved the twigs that held it down. Pam lifted the lamb out of its prison.

"Oh, that poor little thing," said Anna.

"The ewe must have had triplets," said Lulu.

"She had so many babies she probably forgot this one," said Pam. "Let's bring it to her."

"Lightning knew there was an animal in trouble," said Lulu. "She wasn't spooked by the fence after all."

"Good work, Lightning," Pam said to

her pony. Anna hitched Lightning to the fence post and joined Pam and Lulu in the pen.

Pam checked over the tiny newborn. "It's shivering," she said. "And it's full of scratches from the branches." Pam ran her hands gently along the lamb's legs. "I don't think it broke any bones."

Lulu took off her jacket and held it out for Pam. "Here," she said. "Wrap it in this."

Pam put Lulu's jacket around the lamb and carried it toward its mother. The ewe looked up at the girls and bleated as if to say, "Go away. Can't you see I'm busy with my two new babies?"

"She doesn't know that she had three babies," said Anna.

"What are *you* doing here?" someone shouted. The Pony Pals looked up. Mrs. Stewart was coming toward them. "I told you to stay away from here," she said angrily. "This is really too —" Suddenly Mrs. Stewart noticed the ewe with two new-

borns. "Oh, Queenie!" she exclaimed. "I came home because I was worried about you, and look what you've done. Twins!"

"Actually, she had triplets," said Pam. She opened the folds of Lulu's jackets to show Mrs. Stewart the other newborn.

"It's scratched," Mrs. Stewart said. "And cold. I knew there'd be nothing but trouble if children came around here." She took the lamb from Pam.

"We saved this lamb," Anna explained. "It was trapped in the bushes."

"Pam's pony found it," said Lulu.

"And we weren't trespassing," added Pam. "We were on the part of the trail that isn't yours. But when Lightning found the lamb we trespassed to help."

"We love animals, Mrs. Stewart," said Lulu. "We wouldn't do anything to hurt them."

The newborn lamb made the sad, bleating sound again. "I better warm this one up and put iodine on its scratches," Mrs. Stewart said. "And Queenie needs water and hay. Three babies! She must be so thirsty."

"Can we help?" asked Lulu.

Mrs. Stewart looked from one girl to the other. "Well, yes, I guess I could use a little help right now," she said quietly. "Thank you."

"I can help you with those scratches," said Pam. "Lightning has scratches sometimes. My dad showed me what to do."

"We could feed Queenie," said Anna. "And give her water."

"And we'll keep an eye on the other two lambs," added Lulu.

Mrs. Stewart told Anna and Lulu where to go for the water and hay.

Then she and Pam walked to the house. Pam followed her into the kitchen. Mrs. Stewart handed the newborn back to Pam. Pam held the lamb while Mrs. Stewart put iodine on its scratches.

"I'm sorry I yelled at you girls," Mrs. Stewart told Pam. "I've been so worried about the sheep. They acted unusually nervous when we first moved them here. I was afraid we would have problems with the births."

"I understand," said Pam. "I worry about my pony a lot, too."

Now Pam was worried about the little lamb. Would its mother be able to take care of three babies?

A Job for Woolie

Anna and Lulu were sitting on the fence near the ewe. Queenie was standing and the two newborns were on their feet, too. "She ate a lot of hay and drank two buckets of water," Lulu told Mrs. Stewart.

"Thank you," said Mrs. Stewart. Pam carried the lamb toward Queenie. "Leave the jacket there, too," whispered Mrs. Stewart. "The only way Queenie will accept him is if she recognizes his smell. The jacket must have picked up a lot of his scent."

Pam put the lamb and jacket down in front of Queenie.

Queenie took one look at the lamb and walked away from him. The two newborns followed her. The lamb left behind trembled and bleated sadly. "*Maa-maa.*"

Queenie turned and looked again at the lost lamb. "*Maa-maa,*" it bleated again.

"That one is yours, too, Queenie," said Mrs. Stewart. "All three are yours. I know it's a surprise, but you need to take care of *three* babies."

Pam thought she heard Queenie sigh.

"Come on Queenie," Mrs. Stewart whispered. She picked up the lamb and Lulu's jacket and brought them closer to the ewe. She put her hand on Queenie's head and rubbed her nose along the little lamb's side and bottom. Finally, Queenie began to lick the baby. She made a deep throaty sound that seemed to say, "You're mine, too. I'll take care of you."

Mrs. Stewart smiled at the girls. "Thanks," she said. Pam noticed that Mrs.

Stewart had tears in her eyes. Then Mrs. Stewart looked at her watch. "I have to go back to work. But first I have to put a lambing pen around Queenie and her babies."

"We'll help you," said Anna.

"Okay," said Mrs. Stewart. "The fencing is in the barn."

Mrs. Stewart and the Pony Pals ran to the barn together. They each carried a length of portable fence back to Queenie and the triplets. Mrs. Stewart showed the girls how to put the fence together.

"I hate being away from the flock," Mrs. Stewart told the girls. "I left work to check on Queenie today. But I can't do that very often."

"We could check on the sheep after school for you," said Pam.

"It would be easy for us," said Anna. "We like to ride our ponies around here anyway."

"Anna and I live at one end of the trail,"

explained Lulu. "And Pam lives at the other end."

"Did you use the trail to go to one another's houses?" asked Mrs. Stewart.

Pam nodded. "And we meet on the trail to start our trail rides on Ms. Wiggins' property," she said.

"Ms. Wiggins is our friend," said Anna. "Sometimes we help with her horse and pony when she's away."

"It would be wonderful if you girls could check on the sheep after school," said Mrs. Stewart. "But I'm afraid I can't afford to hire sheep-sitters."

"You wouldn't have to pay us," said Lulu.

"But it would be nice if we could use our trail again," said Anna. "My dad said he'd put two gates in your sheep pen so we could go through it."

"Anna's father is the best carpenter in Wiggins," added Lulu. "And he said he'd do it for free."

"Your sheep are already used to us,"

said Pam. "And ponies and sheep are good companions, so the sheep won't mind our ponies that much."

"If you girls hadn't found that lamb, he could have died," said Mrs. Stewart. "You saved his life."

"Lightning did it," said Pam.

"You all did your share," said Mrs. Stewart. "The least I can do is allow you to pass through the sheep pen."

"Really?" said Anna. "You'll let us put in the gates?"

"Yes," said Mrs. Stewart.

"And we'll watch your sheep," said Lulu.

"Woolie would like to help, too," said Pam.

"We can try Woolie out," said Mrs. Stewart. She looked from one girl to the other. "I certainly had no idea what smart girls you were when I first saw you," she said. "We have a very good arrangement here." She shook hands with each of the Pony Pals. "Now I'd better get back to work."

As soon as Mrs. Stewart was out of

sight, Pam raised her hand and the Pony Pals hit high fives and whispered, "All right!"

Queenie "*baa-aa*'d" and her three lambs "*maa-aa*'d."

Lulu pointed up the trail. "Look who's coming!" she exclaimed. Pam saw Woolie running toward them. Lightning nickered a hello to his friend.

"We locked him in the barn this morning," said Pam. "Now how did he get out?"

"Woolie the Wonder Dog!" laughed Anna.

Woolie crawled under the fence and into the pen. Pam grabbed him by the collar. "Slow down," she told him. "And treat these sheep very gently. You have some new lambs to take care of and you don't want to scare them."

Some of the sheep looked in Woolie's direction and a few huddled together. But they didn't seem to be afraid of him. So Pam let him go. Woolie walked around the pen, noticed the newborn lambs, and sat near the fence where he could keep an eye on all of them at once.

"Woolie finally has a job," Pam said.

"And we have our trail back," said Lulu.

"Thanks to Lightning," added Anna.

The Pony Pals climbed the fence and went over to Lightning. Pam put her arms around her pony's neck and gave her a big hug. "You helped save Pony Pal Trail," she told her pony. "Thank you."

Dear Reader:

I am having a lot of fun researching and writing books about the Pony Pals. I've met many interesting kids and adults who love ponies. And I've visited some wonderful ponies at homes, farms, and riding schools.

Before writing Pony Pals I wrote fourteen novels for children and young adults. Four of these were honored by Children's Choice Awards.

I live in Sharon, Connecticut, with my husband, Lee, and our dog, Willie. Our daughter is all grown up and has her own apartment in New York City.

Besides writing novels I like to draw, paint, garden, and swim. I didn't have a pony when I was growing up, but I have always loved them and dreamt about riding. Now I take riding lessons on a horse named Saz.

I like reading and writing about ponies as much as I do riding. Which proves to me that you don't have to ride a pony to love them. And you certainly don't need a pony to be a Pony Pal.

Happy Reading,

Jeanne Betancourt